Doc McStuffins
Chilly Catches a Cold

By Sheila Sweeny Higginson

Based on an episode by Sharon Soboil and Chris Nee

Based on the series created by Chris Nee

Illustrated by Character Building Studio and the Disney Storybook Artists

DISNEY PRESS

New York • Los Angeles

The morning sun shines through Doc's bedroom window.
Doc yawns and rubs her eyes.

2

She sees something sparkling on the trees outside.
"SNOW!" Doc cheers as she dances around.

Doc grabs her stethoscope.
It glows and her toys come to life.
They scramble up to the window.

"Doc!" Chilly cries. "Somebody erased the grass!"
Doc giggles. "Chilly, haven't you ever seen real snow before?"

5

"I've seen snow," Chilly says. "Just not up close."
"Well, what are we waiting for?" asks Stuffy.
"Let's go play in the snow!" Doc says.

She grabs her toys and races through the kitchen.

"Hold on, Doc," her dad says.

He hands Doc her coat, mittens, and scarf so she can bundle up.

"This is amazing!" Chilly says, stepping into the snow.
The other toys agree.

8

Stuffy makes a snow dragon-angel.
Lambie makes a snow princess.

Then the toys decide to make a snow friend for Chilly.
Lambie rolls a big snowball.
Stuffy and Chilly help out, too.

Doc uses stones to make the snow friend's eyes and mouth.
She gives him a carrot nose.
Then she runs inside to get him a hat and scarf.

When Doc returns, Lambie and Stuffy are shivering. It's so cold!
Lambie cuddles up to her.

"Sorry, guys," Doc says. "I should have bundled you up when we went outside."

13

Doc grabs Lambie and Stuffy and heads inside.
"Come on, Chilly," she calls.

"I don't need to get warm," Chilly says.
"I'm made for snow! I'll stay here with my new friend."

Chilly tells jokes to his new friend.
"What do snowmen eat for lunch?" he asks.
"Icebergers!"

But soon Chilly starts to feel like an iceberger himself!
He gets so cold that he can't stop shaking.

Doc gets worried when she comes back and sees her frozen friend.
"We need to get you to the clinic!" she says.

When they get inside, Doc gives Chilly a checkup.
"Do you have a diagnosis, Doc?" asks Hallie.

"Chilly has Brrrr-itis," Doc says.
She asks the toys for their help.

They all cuddle Chilly and try to make him warm again.
"It feels good to get a hug," Chilly says. "It's like the best medicine ever!"

Once Chilly warms up, he feels much better. He's ready to go back outside and play with his snow friend.

"Wait!" Doc calls. "You need to put on warm clothes first."

"Cold weather is no joke," says Doc. "Everyone—even stuffed snowmen—should dress warm for cold weather."

Now that Chilly is bundled up in his warm clothes, he can play in the snow all day.
"What does a snowman put on his head?" he asks his snow friend.
"An ice cap!"